The Butterflies' Promise

The Butterflies' Promise

by Julie Ovenell-Carter   illustrations by Kitty Macaulay

Annick Press
Toronto • New York • Vancouver

We acknowledge the support of the Canada Council for the Arts
for our publishing program. We also thank the Ontario Arts Council.

THE CANADA COUNCIL | LE CONSEIL DES ARTS
FOR THE ARTS | DU CANADA
SINCE 1957 | DEPUIS 1957

Cataloguing in Publication Data

Ovenell-Carter, Julie
  The butterflies' promise

ISBN 1-55037-567-9 (bound) ISBN 1-55037-566-0 (pbk.)

I. Macaulay, Kitty. II. Title.

PS8579.V44B87 1999   jC813'.54   C98-932597-0
PZ7.O93Bu 1999

The art in this book was rendered in water-colours.
The text was typeset in Slimbach.

Distributed in Canada by:
Firefly Books Ltd.
3680 Victoria Park Avenue
Willowdale, ON
M2H 3K1

Published in the U.S.A. by Annick Press (U.S.) Ltd.
Distributed in the U.S.A. by:
Firefly Books (U.S.) Inc.
P.O. Box 1338
Ellicott Station
Buffalo, NY 14205

Printed and bound in Canada by
Friesens, Altona, Manitoba

... these are flowers that fly and all but sing ...
—Robert Frost

To my grandmothers, Christina and Alwin
—J.O-C.

*For Love, which even in
difficult times brings joy*
—K.M.

Milly's grandpa had a garden bigger than a city block. Everywhere you looked, tomatoes spilled off trellises and pumpkins plumped in the sun. There were rose-bushes and bush beans and bushy little strawberries always ready with a treat. But the best thing was the butterflies. Grandpa's flying flowers, Milly called them.

"Do you think it's the same ones that come back every year?" Milly asked Grandpa as they sat shelling peas one hot afternoon.

"I don't really know," said Grandpa. "But I like to think it's their children and their children's children who keep visiting us."

"If I was a butterfly, *I* would come back to this garden," said Milly, rolling peas into a pot with her thumb.

Grandpa, laughing, hung pea shells over Milly's ears. "Here are your wings, little butterfly. Promise me you'll always come back."

Milly helped Grandpa long into the fall. One morning, she saw he was carrying all the bird feeders to the storage shed.

"Don't put them away!" cried Milly. "We need to hang them for winter."

"Now Milly," said Grandpa, "I'm feeling too creaky to be climbing any ladders. I'm afraid I might just tip right over into that pile of leaves."

"Then let me do it," said Milly, taking the feeders from Grandpa's arms.

Later, they rested, stretched like sleeping cats under the soft autumn sun. A small orange cloud floated past.

"It's the monarchs," said Grandpa. "They're on their way south for the winter. We'll see them again next spring."

There was snow on the ground the day Milly's grandpa got sick. When Milly came home from school, her mother gathered Milly into her lap and told her what had happened.

"Grandpa was taken to the hospital in an ambulance. It's hard for him to talk right now, and he can't walk. But we hope it won't be very long before he can come home again."

Milly picked at her sweater. "Can I see him?"

"Soon," said Mom. "He's still very sleepy. But maybe if you drew him a picture, we could hang it by his bed and he would know you were thinking of him."

Milly drew so many pictures that the nurses
could hardly find Grandpa in his bed.

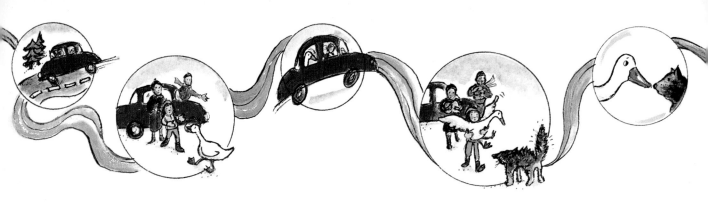

Finally, spring came. Milly was learning a song for Grandpa, a dance he liked when he was a little boy. She tried to concentrate, but she could hear her mom talking on the telephone to Milly's aunt. Her mother was crying. She was talking about Grandpa.

"He won't be able to live by himself any more," said her mother. "He'll need some very special care."

At dinner, Milly said to her mother, "I heard you talking on the phone today. I know a place where the people will take really good care of Grandpa."

"Where is that, Milly?"

"Here. Grandpa can live right here with us. I'll share my bedroom."

Her dad sighed. "Oh, Milly. It *would* be wonderful if Grandpa could be with us all the time, but he needs to live in a special place, where there will always be someone to look after him. Grandpa needs lots of help now—someone to help him get dressed, eat and move around. He even needs help to go to the bathroom."

"But no one loves Grandpa as much as we do," cried Milly. "*We* have to do something."

"Then I'll tell you what we'll do," said Dad, hugging her close. "We'll help Grandpa the best way we can. We'll go visit."

When the day came to visit Grandpa,
Milly was still sad. "I don't think I want to go.
It just won't be the same without our garden."

Her dad sat beside her on the stoop. "You
know, I was thinking the same thing last
night. I was thinking, 'I don't believe I can
live through a whole summer without a bas-
ket of Grandpa's strawberries.' And then
all of a sudden a plan popped into my
head. Do you want to hear it?"

Milly listened. She smiled.
"Hurry," she said, "let's go!"

Grandpa's new home was a big white building way across town. He was already waiting by the door when Milly arrived. He held tightly to her little hand while Milly's dad pushed him into the sunny courtyard. While her parents talked quietly with Grandpa, Milly explored.

She found a bright orange monarch resting against the trunk of a big old beech tree. Gently, she cupped it in her hands and brought it back to Grandpa.

"Look, I have a surprise for you!" said Milly, letting the butterfly go. Grandpa clapped his hand to his knee and smiled.

"This place could use a few more butterflies," said Milly's dad, looking around the flowerless court-yard. "What do you think, Milly? Can we help Grandpa do something about that?"

"We've got a plan!" laughed Milly.

Soon, Grandpa had a new garden. Milly's father built garden beds around the edge of the courtyard, high enough that Grandpa could reach them from his wheelchair.

Milly's mother brought special
tools to make it easier for Grandpa
to dig. Milly brought buckets of
compost from her own backyard.
In no time, there were
other people who
wanted to help.

And the butterflies came.

At the end of the summer, Grandpa decided there should be a party to share his small harvest. Milly picked flowers to decorate the tables.

After dinner, there was a concert. When Milly played Grandpa's favourite song, her mom danced him around the dining hall.

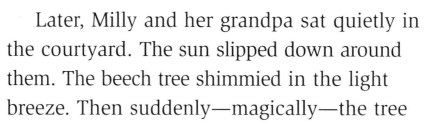

Later, Milly and her grandpa sat quietly in the courtyard. The sun slipped down around them. The beech tree shimmied in the light breeze. Then suddenly—magically—the tree burst into flames, glowing orange in the near-night.

They watched as the tree changed from orange to green to orange again, like a giant kaleidoscope.

And then Milly understood.

"It's the monarchs," she whispered. "They're getting ready to fly away for the winter."

A thousand silken wings waved across the dim sky and then exploded into the air, a bouquet tossed heavenward,

Grandpa's flying flowers.

Monarchs gather in groups in the fall, as far north as Canada. They migrate south to spend the winter in California or Mexico. They can cover long distances in one day, flying at great speeds and heights. When they stop to rest, they can cover entire trees.

In the spring, when they journey north again, the females search for milkweed on which to lay their eggs. Because these eggs hatch into caterpillars that eat only milkweed leaves, it's important for the monarch mothers to find this plant.

When the caterpillar becomes a butterfly, it no longer has a mouth. Instead, it has a long, straw-like tongue that it can uncurl to sip nectar from flowers. Butterflies like any bright-coloured flower in full sun, but their favourite colours are red and yellow. They prefer old-fashioned flowers that have kept their scent and nectar. They are wild about tubular blossoms, like those of lantana, because these make the most comfortable butterfly chairs.

To have butterflies visit, plant the flowers they love most:

- butterfly weed (a type of milkweed)
- wild milkweed (gather seed from pods in the fall)
- bushes such as butterfly bush and California buckwheat
- flowers such as cosmos, lantana, Shasta daisy and zinnia

Butterflies are very gentle with children. They don't sting or bite. It's fun to have one land on you. They are more likely to do this if you are wearing light-coloured clothing and stand very still.

If you want to know more about butterflies, there are great books at the library.

—K.M.